Anna, Banana,

and the
Big-Mouth
Bet

Anna, Banana,

and the
Big-Mouth
Bet

~~~~~~~

Anica Mrose Rissi

ILLUSTRATED BY **Meg Park**

~~~~~~~

SIMON & SCHUSTER
BOOKS FOR YOUNG READERS
New York London Toronto Sydney New Delhi

SIMON & SCHUSTER BOOKS FOR YOUNG READERS
An imprint of Simon & Schuster Children's Publishing Division
1230 Avenue of the Americas, New York, New York 10020

For information about special discounts for bulk purchases, please contact Simon & Schuster Special Sales at 1-866-506-1949 or business@simonandschuster.com.
The Simon & Schuster Speakers Bureau can bring authors to your live event. For more information or to book an event, contact the Simon & Schuster Speakers Bureau at 1-866-248-3049 or visit our website at www.simonspeakers.com.
Book design by Laurent Linn
The text for this book is set in Minister Std.
The illustrations for this book are rendered digitally.
Manufactured in the United States of America
0815 FFG
2 4 6 8 10 9 7 5 3 1
Library of Congress Cataloging-in-Publication Data
Rissi, Anica Mrose.
Anna, Banana, and the big-mouth bet / Anica Mrose Rissi ;
illustrated by Meg Park. — First edition.
pages cm
Summary: After telling her dog Banana about her loose tooth and discovering that some of her friends do not believe in the Tooth Fairy, Anna makes an impulsive bet with a pesky boy who also has a loose tooth.
ISBN 978-1-4814-1611-5 (hardcover)
ISBN 978-1-4814-1613-9 (eBook)
[1. Teeth—Fiction. 2. Tooth Fairy—Fiction. 3. Wagers—Fiction. 4. Friendship—Fiction. 5. Dogs—Fiction.] I. Park, Meg, illustrator. II. Title.
PZ7.R5265Al 2015
[Fic]—dc23
2014031600

FIRST
EDITION

For Jeremy
(Wanna play trash compactor?)
—A. M. R.

To us who believe in magic
—M. P.

Chapter One
That Spells Trouble

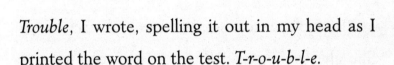

Trouble, I wrote, spelling it out in my head as I printed the word on the test. *T-r-o-u-b-l-e*.

O-plus-*U* and *L*-before-*E* were the hard parts in that one, but I was certain I'd gotten it right. Dad had quizzed me on all the spelling and vocabulary words this morning at breakfast, and even Banana was amazed by how quickly I'd breezed through them. And dogs are hardly ever impressed by good spelling.

I tapped my lucky blue pencil against my lip as I thought about how to use the word in a sentence. *Banana once got in trouble for chewing*

Chuck's sneaker, I wrote, wrinkling my nose at the memory. Banana doesn't chew on things she's not supposed to anymore, but she still loves sniffing at things that stink, including my older brother's yucky shoes.

"Pesky!" our teacher, Ms. Burland, exclaimed. She always sings out the words for our tests as though she's performing them onstage. It makes the quizzes a lot more dramatic, and even kind of fun. "Pesky," she repeated, this time in a low, booming voice. Beside me, my best friend Isabel giggled.

I wrote down the word, then used it in a sentence: *Those pesky flies won't leave us alone!*

I glanced over at my other best friend, Sadie. I knew she'd been nervous about the test, so I was worried for her. But Sadie was bent over her paper, scribbling the answer, with her curls spilling into her face. It looked like she was doing fine.

"No cheating, Anna!" Justin called out from the desk behind mine. My mouth fell open and my heart sped up at the attack. I wasn't cheating!

Ms. Burland raised her eyebrows in our direction. "You should all have your eyes on your own papers, please," she said.

I looked down quickly. I wasn't really in trouble, but my cheeks still burned. Forget flies—I should have written my sentence about pesky Justin. He was the worst.

"Accuse," Ms. Burland announced, sounding stern. "Accuse!" she repeated, calling it out like a cheerful greeting.

I narrowed my eyes. *Justin likes to accuse innocent girls of cheating*, I wrote on my test. There. That ought to clear my name. And I hoped Ms. Burland would notice that I'd also used one of last week's spelling words, "innocent," and spelled it correctly. I thought that was pretty clever of me.

But wait, was "cheat-ing" spelled right? I pressed my lips together, thinking hard, and gasped. I'd felt a tooth move! I touched the tooth with my tongue and pushed it again. Sure enough, it wiggled.

I was so distracted by the slightly loose tooth, I almost missed the final spelling word. Luckily, Ms. Burland said it once more. "About."

I spelled it out carefully and wrote, *I can't wait to tell Banana and Sadie and Isabel about my loose tooth!*

Chapter Two
Loosey-Goosey

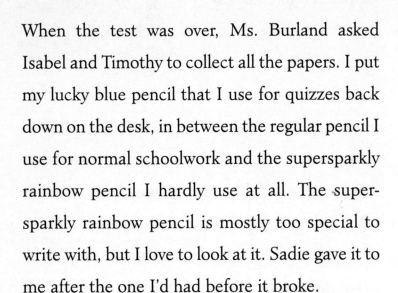

When the test was over, Ms. Burland asked Isabel and Timothy to collect all the papers. I put my lucky blue pencil that I use for quizzes back down on the desk, in between the regular pencil I use for normal schoolwork and the supersparkly rainbow pencil I hardly use at all. The supersparkly rainbow pencil is mostly too special to write with, but I love to look at it. Sadie gave it to me after the one I'd had before it broke.

I peeked over at Sadie and lifted both eyebrows to ask, *How'd the test go?* Sadie grinned and gave me a thumbs-up.

Usually Theresa, the housekeeper at Sadie's mom's place, helps Sadie study for spelling tests. But this week Theresa was away on vacation and Sadie was staying at her dad's house, and he's not as good as my dad or Theresa at quiz prep. He does buy us really tasty snacks for sleepovers, though. And he lets us drink soda and watch TV, and doesn't get mad about pillow fights.

There's no soda allowed at my house, and it's hard to get away with a late-night pillow fight because Banana gets excited and wakes everyone up with her barking. Though my dad said even if Banana hadn't barked, he still would have heard Sadie and Isabel and me shrieking and giggling at the sleepover last weekend. Now that I have two best friends, we make a lot more noise than when I only had one.

The bell rang for recess and we lined up to follow Ms. Burland down the hall. Sadie, Isabel, and I ran straight for the small merry-go-round as soon as we got outside. Usually third graders don't go on the small merry-go-round because it's made for little kids, but we wanted to play a new game Isabel had invented called Spin Me a Tale.

The game is, one person sits in the center of the merry-go-round and holds on to the bars while the other two spin her around. As the person is spinning, she has to make up a story and tell it really quick, before the merry-go-round slows to a stop. But spinning on the merry-go-round makes our brains dizzy, so the stories usually come out pretty silly.

If someone shouts "Switch!" we spin the merry-go-round in the other direction, and the storyteller has to switch something important about the story—the evil fairy becomes good, or the puppy turns into a goose, or the princess doesn't want to marry the prince after all. Switch is my favorite part.

Yesterday I made up a story about Banana chasing a squirrel made of cheese, and when

Isabel yelled "Switch!" I changed it to the cheese chasing Banana. We laughed so hard that Isabel snorted. Justin heard the snort and started making piggy noises, which only made Isabel laugh even harder, but Sadie still told him to go away. Sadie likes Justin and sometimes giggles at his jokes, but she doesn't like anyone making fun of her friends.

I felt like Justin had been giving us an extra-hard time this week. I wished I knew how to get him to bug off.

"Whose turn is it?" Isabel asked as we reached the merry-go-round. We try to take turns and be fair with games and stuff.

"Mine!" Sadie said, climbing into the middle.

"Wait," I said. "I have something to show you. Look!" I dropped open my jaw and wiggled the loose tooth with my finger. It was a bottom tooth—one of the extra-pointy ones.

"Oooooh, loose tooth!" Isabel said.

Sadie peered in closer. "I don't see anything," she said.

"It isn't super loose yet," I explained. "But it will be."

Isabel bounced on her toes. Her face was full of excitement. "I wonder what the Tooth Fairy will bring you," she said.

I shrugged. "I usually get a few coins and a treat, like sparkly stickers or a cool hair tie."

"Isn't it funny how the Tooth Fairy brings different things to different houses?" Isabel said. "I always get a letter with my prize, but my friend Cassie from Ms. Lahiri's class last year only gets money. Maybe it's because I leave the Tooth Fairy a note and a drawing along with my tooth, so she writes back."

I squinted at her. Sometimes it's hard to tell if Isabel is joking. Chuck had told Sadie and me the truth about the Tooth Fairy years ago. Surely Isabel's big sisters would have told her by now too. But Isabel looked completely serious.

I glanced at Sadie, expecting her to inform Isabel that there is no Tooth Fairy, but Sadie went with it. "The Tooth Fairy comes to *both* my houses," she said. "Last time I got money under the pillow at my mom's house and a whole box of chocolate caramels plus a letter at my dad's."

I remembered those chocolates. They'd been

delicious. Sadie and
I had shared one
every day for the next
two weeks, at whatever
random moment Sadie
had declared it to be Chocolate

Time. That was before we became friends with
Isabel. I've known Sadie forever, but we only just
met Isabel in Ms. Burland's class this year.

If Sadie wasn't going to say anything to Isabel
about the Tooth Fairy, then I wouldn't either. But
it was kind of embarrassing that she didn't know
the truth.

"Let's play the game," I said to change the
subject. I'd spotted our classmates Amanda and
Keisha skipping rope nearby. They didn't look
like they were listening to us, but I didn't want

to risk them overhearing. If they caught on that Isabel still believed in the Tooth Fairy, they might think she was babyish. What if they thought I was babyish too?

Not that it mattered what Amanda thought—she sometimes picks her nose in public—but who knew who she'd tell. If Justin found out, he would never let us hear the end of it. The last thing we needed was more teasing from him.

"Spin me!" Sadie commanded.

Isabel and I grabbed on to the merry-go-round and the story began.

Chapter Three
More Than a Mouthful

I showed Banana my loose tooth first thing after school, before clipping on her leash for our walk around the block, and I wiggled it with my finger all through doing my homework, to try to make it even looser. It seemed to be working. By dinner-time I could move it back and forth in the same rhythm as Banana wagging her tail.

Dad walked into the kitchen, where I was finishing up my fractions and division worksheet and Banana was finishing a nap in a sunbeam. "Hey, kiddo. Hey, dog-o," he said as he took off the tie he always wears while he writes and put on the apron that Mom gave him last Christmas. It's red, his favorite color, and the front says, STIRRING UP TROUBLE.

"Hey, Dad-o," I said back.

Dad lifted the lid off a pot that was heating on the stove, and I caught a whiff of something delicious. Banana smelled it too and went over to stand near Dad's feet, in case he decided to drop her a taste.

"If you go tell your brother and your mother, 'Dinner in ten minutes,' I'll let you off the hook on helping set the table tonight," Dad said as he took four plates out of the cabinet.

"Deal!" I said, jumping up fast before he could change his mind. Ten minutes was also long enough to watch the baby horse video Sadie had been telling me and Isabel about, if Mom would let me borrow her phone.

When I came back downstairs after seeing the video twice, a giant bowl of yummy spaghetti was sitting in the center of the dinner table. Unfortunately, so was a bowl of brussels sprouts.

Banana and I do not like brussels sprouts.

At least it wasn't beets, which I hate so much that Chuck always specially requests them for his birthday dinner, just so I'll have to eat them that night.

I knew Banana was disappointed that there were no turkey meatballs that might roll off the spaghetti and into her mouth, but she still watched hopefully as Dad heaped the noodles and tomato sauce onto our plates. I wrinkled my nose as he put a scoop of brussels sprouts on my plate too, but I knew better than to object. My parents love launching into the "In This House, You Eat What You're Served" lecture. Thank goodness it was just a small helping.

I pushed my brussels sprouts around in the tomato sauce, hoping that might cover up the taste, as Chuck told us about a home run he almost got during kickball in gym class, except in the end he was tagged out instead.

"Anna, how was the spelling test?" Mom asked when Chuck's story was finished. She passed me the loaf of garlic bread and I took a big slice. Dad's garlic bread is delicious.

"Great," I said, deciding not to mention how Justin had accused me of cheating. "I think I spelled everything right. And I got a loose tooth!" I opened my mouth to show them the tooth and how much it wiggled. It was already much looser than it had been at school.

"Uh-oh," Dad said. "You weren't supposed to *chew* on the test." I giggled.

"Yeah," Chuck said. "Next time just lick it, or soon you'll be toothless."

I kicked Chuck under the table. He stretched his lips over his teeth and said, "Hi, I'm Anna, and I have no teeth," but it came out sounding like, "Hi, I'm Amma, am I hab mo peepf."

Banana barked in my defense.

"When all your teeth fall out, you'll only be able to eat mushy foods, like fish brains and gruel," Chuck said. "Also, mashed beets. Mmm."

I stuck out my tongue at him. "No, I'll eat nothing but ice cream," I said. "You can keep your stinky fish brains."

Chuck laughed and sucked in his cheeks to make a fish face at me, but Mom shot both of us a stern look. We're not supposed to fight at the dinner table.

Luckily, Dad came to the rescue. "Do you know what those pointy teeth like your loose one are called? Canines!"

"That means 'dog,'" Chuck said with his mouth full. He swallowed before anyone could scold him, and gave me a wicked grin. "So maybe when the tooth falls out, you'll be less of one."

"Chuck!" Mom said. "That's enough. Don't be mean to your sister."

But I didn't mind being called a dog. I knew Chuck meant it as an insult, but I love dogs. Being a dog would be great.

If I were a dog, I could nap in a sunbeam and play tug-of-war and chase butterflies and squirrels with Banana all day. I'd never have to do homework or chores, or eat brussels sprouts, and if Justin came along and bothered me, I could bite him. Or at least bark and growl at him until he went away.

I'd miss Isabel and Sadie while they were at school all day without me, though. And I didn't think I'd like eating dog food. So maybe it was good that I was human, except for my canine teeth.

Chapter Four
Things Get Twisted

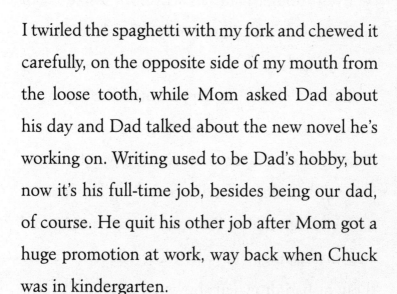

I twirled the spaghetti with my fork and chewed it carefully, on the opposite side of my mouth from the loose tooth, while Mom asked Dad about his day and Dad talked about the new novel he's working on. Writing used to be Dad's hobby, but now it's his full-time job, besides being our dad, of course. He quit his other job after Mom got a huge promotion at work, way back when Chuck was in kindergarten.

Dad says Mom is the family breadwinner, which I guess means she earns all the money for our spaghetti, even though Dad does most of the grocery shopping. He's proud that Mom is the boss at her office, but I don't see what the big deal is. She's kind of the boss at home, too. Banana thinks so, anyway.

Even though Dad has written a whole lot of books that are in libraries and bookstores and everything, he says that each new story still poses a different challenge. Apparently, the big challenge to this one was figuring out what would happen next. Dad says every good novel needs a plot twist, which is when something unexpected happens that makes the story more complicated and interesting, like when the sailor everyone thought had drowned shows up alive, or it turns out the poor servant girl is really a princess.

Figuring out a plot twist sounded a lot like playing Spin Me a Tale. I thought maybe Dad should try writing his books on a merry-go-round.

"I've got an idea. Aliens invade!" Chuck said. "That'd be a plot twist no one saw coming."

"That *would* be surprising," Dad said, "since this is supposed to be a historical romance novel."

"Aliens are very romantic," Chuck said. We all cracked up.

"The girl could fall in love with a caveman," I suggested. "That's historical. Or, wait, at first she doesn't like him at all, but then she *caves in*. Get it?"

Chuck snorted. Mom smiled. Dad shook his head.

I looked down at Banana and she nudged my foot with her snout. She was still hoping for the kind of plot twist where someone drops an entire plate of spaghetti on the floor so she can eat it.

But by now all our plates were empty. I'd even managed to swallow down the brussels sprouts, thanks to my tomato sauce trick.

"Maybe the hero gets a loose tooth and he falls in love with the Tooth Fairy," I said as Chuck and I stood up to clear the table.

"And they get married and go live in a castle made of teeth," Mom said.

"Yeah, and host imaginary tea parties with the Abominable Snowman and the Loch Ness Monster and Bigfoot as their guests," Chuck added.

Even Dad laughed at that one. Chuck is pretty funny sometimes.

"Well, thanks, family," Dad said, pretending to take our jokes seriously. "That should be enough twists for the next three or four books."

Mom kissed him on the cheek. "Should we celebrate with dessert?" she said. "I brought home some ice cream."

That sounded like the best idea of all.

Chapter Five
Toothy Trouble

The next morning Mom drove us to school on her way to work so that Chuck wouldn't have to walk carrying the project he'd made for history class. It was a diorama of the insides of an ancient Egyptian pyramid, and it looked really cool. Chuck had drawn real hieroglyphics on the walls, and Banana and I had helped by wrapping a plastic doll in thin strips of toilet paper to turn it into a mummy. I bet it would be the best diorama in the whole sixth grade.

When we got to school, I found Isabel out on the playground, sitting on a rock near the swings with her nose in a book. She looked up and smiled when she saw me. "Hi!" I said. "Where's Sadie?"

Isabel shrugged. "Her bus isn't here yet."

"Whatcha reading?" I plopped down on the rock next to her and peeked over her shoulder.

Isabel reads about a million books a week. Her three older sisters are bookworms too, and her Abuelita is a librarian, so her house is full of good books. The one she was reading today had a spooky graveyard on the cover. "I started it last night," she said. "It's not as scary as it looks, but it's pretty good so far. How's your tooth?"

"Much looser," I said. I wiggled it to demonstrate.

Isabel closed her book and beamed at me. "Soon the Tooth Fairy will come!" she singsonged.

I grinned. "Yeah, right after she finishes her tea party with Bigfoot and the Abominable Snowman and all her other imaginary friends," I said, repeating Chuck's joke.

Instead of laughing, Isabel blinked in surprise. She looked as stunned and confused as Banana did that time when I accidentally stepped on her tail.

I swallowed hard, wishing I could gulp down the words. Somehow that had sounded much funnier when Chuck had said it. When I'd said it, it just sounded mean. Like the kind of thing Justin might say. Like I was making fun of her for still believing.

"I'm sorry," I said. "That came out wrong."

Isabel looked down. "Okay," she said. "I don't know why you'd say that, though."

The back of my neck prickled with shame. I wished I could jump on the merry-go-round and spin us backwards to turn back time and undo hurting her feelings. I just hadn't been thinking.

"It was a joke. A dumb joke. But, Isabel . . ." Since Isabel had brought it up, I had to tell her the truth. "You know there's no Tooth Fairy, right?"

Isabel stared at me for what felt like a long time. I couldn't tell what she was thinking.

"No," she finally said. "I don't know that. I know some people believe that, but I don't think it's true."

"What's not true?" Sadie asked, coming up behind us.

"Nothing," I said quickly.

"The Tooth Fairy," Isabel said. I held my breath and waited for Sadie to repeat the truth.

"Oh," Sadie said. "Guess what? My dad says I can have you guys over after school tomorrow. We can take turns riding my new bike."

Isabel brightened. "Cool," she said.

"Cool," I echoed. But it didn't fix what I'd said to Isabel.

I should have kept my big mouth shut.

Chapter Six

Birds of a Feather

Even the worst Wednesday morning always gets better, because on Wednesdays we start the day with art.

This morning Ms. Burland showed us one of her favorite artists, Charley Harper, who made a lot of cool-looking birds. We talked about what Ms. Burland called his "geometric style," meaning that the birds are made out of bold, simple shapes like triangles and squares and circles and half circles, all layered and pieced together. Then we took out glue and scissors and colored paper,

and got to work, cutting out shapes for our own bird collages.

One of the images Ms. Burland showed us had all these long, thin rectangles that looked like branches.

I wanted to try that on my collage, so I picked a sheet of bright blue paper to use for the background and some light-gray paper to cut into tree strips.

First, though, I got a piece of pretty yellow paper and cut it into a heart. I wrote *I'm sorry* on one side of the heart and drew a picture of Banana on the other side, with two little lines near her tail to show she was wagging it. Once I saw that Ms. Burland wasn't watching, I passed the heart to Isabel at the desk next to mine.

I was pretty sure I'd done the right thing by telling Isabel the truth about the Tooth Fairy, even though she hadn't wanted to believe it. *Somebody* had to tell her, and it was better that she hear it from a friend. But I really was sorry for what I'd said before that—for accidentally making fun of her by repeating Chuck's stupid joke. I wanted her to know I felt bad about it.

Isabel looked at the note and smiled at me, and I sighed with relief. I vowed that from that moment on, I was going to be nothing but a truly good friend to her and Sadie both.

I got to work on my collage, pushing at my loose tooth with my tongue while I glued down the trees for my background and cut out red and black shapes to use for my bird.

"Very nice," Ms. Burland said as she passed

by my desk in her tall, shiny boots with buttons all up the sides. I sat up straighter. "Great color choices," she said to Isabel.

I looked over at Isabel's collage as Ms. Burland crossed to the other side of the room. Isabel's black-and-white bird was floating in a lake of dark-purple water, with a lavender sky and a fuchsia moon above it. It looked amazing, which was no surprise. Isabel is the best artist in our class. I felt a flash of pride that she was one of my two best friends.

"It's a loon," she said shyly.

Before I could respond, Justin butted in. "A loon?" he said. "I didn't realize we were doing self-portraits."

Isabel's eyes went wide. I turned around to glare at Justin.

"What's yours, Anna, a cuckoo bird?" he said.

"No!" I said, wishing I could think of a better response.

"Cuckoo! Cuckoo!" Justin crowed. My whole face felt hot.

Suddenly Sadie was there between us with her hands on her hips. "Justin Chan, you leave my friends alone," she said. "You know who makes fun of people like that? A big *chicken*."

She turned and marched back to her desk before Justin could say another word.

Surprisingly, he *didn't* say another word, to either Isabel or me, for the entire rest of the morning. He didn't even kick my chair.

Isabel passed me a note: *Sadie is a superhero.*

I nodded. It was true, and I loved Sadie for it.

But I also felt a tiny bit jealous. I wanted to

be the kind of friend who saves the day, instead of being the one who'd almost ruined it. But I hadn't done anything to stick up for Isabel. I hadn't even been able to defend myself.

Chapter Seven

A Lot to Swallow

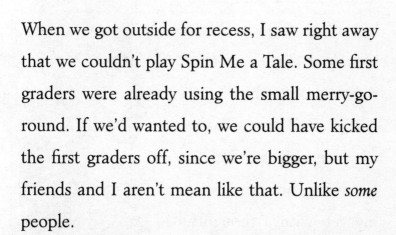

When we got outside for recess, I saw right away that we couldn't play Spin Me a Tale. Some first graders were already using the small merry-go-round. If we'd wanted to, we could have kicked the first graders off, since we're bigger, but my friends and I aren't mean like that. Unlike *some* people.

"Let's take the swings," Sadie said, so we ran there instead.

"What are we going to do about Justin? He's so annoying," I said as I pushed off the ground.

Sadie shrugged, kicking off too. "He's not

always that bad. He just sometimes doesn't know when to stop."

"I don't want him to even *start*," I said. I pumped my legs to go higher. "You're lucky you don't have to sit right in front of him."

I glanced over at Isabel, who was sitting quietly on her swing, not even swinging yet, with a thoughtful look on her face. I waited for her to say something about Justin's teasing, but instead she asked, "What makes you so sure there's no Tooth Fairy, Anna?"

My feet hit the ground with a thud and I dragged them in the dirt to bring myself to a stop. Sadie halted her swing too.

"Well," I said as both of them looked at me. "Chuck told us. Back in kindergarten, when I lost my second tooth. We didn't want to believe him, but Sadie said we should check. I put the tooth under my pillow before bed, and my mom came to tuck me in like she always does. But after she left, I put my hand under my pillow and the tooth was already gone. There was a silver dollar and a pack of bubble gum, but the Tooth Fairy couldn't have been there yet. My mom had to have left it."

Isabel tilted her head to the side like Banana does when she's trying to figure something out. "Did you fall asleep while you were waiting to be tucked in?" she asked.

"What? No," I said, trying to remember. "I don't know. Maybe. It was a long time ago. Why?"

"Because it's possible the Tooth Fairy *did* come and take the tooth if you were really tired and fell asleep right away, before your mom came up," Isabel explained.

I hesitated. "I guess so," I said, even though I didn't think that was true. I looked at Sadie for help.

"Probably not," Sadie said as nicely as possible.

"Yeah, probably not," Isabel said, nodding. "Because you already didn't believe."

"What?" I said again. Somehow it was beginning to feel like *I* was the one who didn't know about things. Isabel sounded so calm and sure.

"You didn't believe," Isabel repeated patiently. "Once you stop believing in the Tooth Fairy, the

Tooth Fairy stops coming, so your parents have to take over. That's how the magic works."

Sadie looked skeptical. "How do you know that?" she asked.

Isabel shrugged. "All magic has rules," she said. "There's a certain way you have to do it, or it doesn't work. Like, think about birthday-wish magic. You have to blow out the candles all in one breath, and you have to think of your wish while you're doing it, and you can't tell any-one what you wished for. Otherwise, the magic doesn't work."

"Right," I agreed. I believed in that. Birthday-wish magic was how I'd gotten Banana.

"Well, the rule with the Tooth Fairy's magic is that you have to put the tooth under your pillow before you fall asleep, and you have to believe,"

Isabel said. "If you don't believe, the Tooth Fairy doesn't come."

I stared at her with my mouth open. I'd never thought of it like that.

"It's nice of your parents to step in and pretend, though," she added.

Wow, I thought. I could tell Sadie wasn't convinced by Isabel's theory. But secretly I so, so wanted it to be true.

Chapter Eight
Chew on This

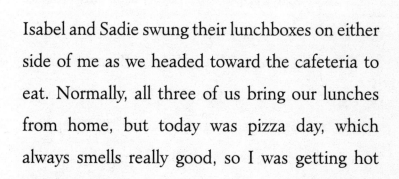

Isabel and Sadie swung their lunchboxes on either side of me as we headed toward the cafeteria to eat. Normally, all three of us bring our lunches from home, but today was pizza day, which always smells really good, so I was getting hot lunch instead.

My friends went over to our usual table by the windows while I stood in line to wait for my food. Jesmyn, who was in Ms. Dandino's class with Sadie and me last year but had Mr. Garrison for third grade this year, got in line behind me. We smiled and said hi. For a second I thought about asking her what she thinks of the Tooth Fairy, but some other kids were lining up behind her and I didn't want them to overhear. It was way too embarrassing.

"Cheese or pepperoni?" the lunch lady asked when I reached the counter.

"Cheese, please," I said, since Banana wasn't there to feed the pepperonis to. Banana loves any pizza toppings, even anchovies, but pepperonis are her favorite. I mostly like my pizza plain.

I took a box of milk from the dairy case and carried my tray toward the spot where my friends were waiting. I was swerving around a bunch of kids all gathered around another table when I heard Justin's voice coming from the middle of the crowd. I heard him say "Tooth!" along with something else, and the whole group laughed.

I froze. *Oh no oh no oh no,* I thought. The worst had happened. He'd heard about Isabel and he was telling everyone and they were all making fun of her and the whole school was laughing.

I had to do something. I had to stop him.

I would not let him do this to my friend.

I took a deep breath and pushed past the other kids, imagining myself wearing tights and a cape. "Enough!" I said, slamming my tray down on Justin's table. "You need to shut your big mouth!"

Chapter Nine
You Bet

Justin jumped in surprise. "What'd I do?" he said.

The fact that he was pretending to be inno-cent made me even madder. "First you made fun of my friend and called her a loon," I said. "Then you made fun of me, too. And now you're . . ." I stopped, suddenly realizing something I hadn't quite processed before. When I'd stormed up to the table, Justin had had his mouth wide open and his finger inside it. He'd been touching his tooth.

Maybe he wasn't telling everyone that Isabel still believed in the Tooth Fairy. Maybe he'd been wiggling and talking about his *own* loose tooth.

Whoops. I clamped my mouth shut. But everyone was staring at me, waiting to hear the end of that sentence. And the longer it took me to finish, the smirkier Justin's smirk was becoming. I had to say *something*.

"Now you're showing off your dumb loose tooth like you're the only one who's ever had one!" I finished lamely.

This was so embarrassing. I wished I could tuck my tail between my legs like Banana and scootch out of there, fast. But it was too late now.

At least Justin was too stunned to respond.

I heard Isabel's voice behind me. "You have a loose tooth?" she said. "So does Anna."

Uh-oh. I needed to jump in fast, before Isabel said something about believing in the Tooth Fairy in front of the entire cafeteria. I could at least save her from that. I blurted out the first words I could think of. "Yeah, but he just got his, so mine is going to fall out first."

That snapped Justin back to life. "Is not," he said.

"Is to," I shot back.

"Says who?"

"Says me!"

"Wanna bet?" he said.

I didn't want to bet on anything with Justin. I just wanted him to stop making fun of me and my friends. But maybe this was my chance for that. Maybe this was a way I could stand up for all of us.

"Fine," I said. "I bet that my tooth will fall out before yours does. And if I'm right, you have to leave me and my friends alone for the entire rest of the year. No more teasing us. No more pestering. No talking to us, or even kicking my chair."

"Fine," Justin said, his smile growing. "And if mine falls out first, then I get your tooth."

"My what?" I shrieked.

"Your tooth," Justin said, looking smug. "If you lose, you have to give me your tooth when it falls out."

"I can't give you my tooth!" I said.

"Why not?" he demanded.

"Because . . ." I didn't know how to explain it, but that just seemed wrong. The idea of anyone having my tooth was icky, but especially if that anyone was Justin. "Because it's mine. Why would you even want it?"

Justin rolled his eyes. "To get more money from the Tooth Fairy," he said, like it should have been obvious.

My mouth dropped open. "That's cheating! And you can't trick the Tooth Fairy." Surely that was true whether the Tooth Fairy was real or not.

Beside me, Isabel was nodding. Sadie stood

close on my other side, making me feel stronger. It was good knowing that my friends had my back.

"I won't give you my tooth," I said to Justin. "Choose something else."

He thought for a minute. "Okay," he said. "If you lose, you have to stand up in the middle of class and dance the Funky Chicken." Justin tucked his hands into his armpits and flapped his elbows to demonstrate. "Bawk, bawk!" he cried.

No way was I doing that during class. Even the idea of it was embarrassing. And Ms. Burland would give me detention for life.

But I wasn't going to

lose this bet anyway. I had to win it, for me and my friends.

"Fine," I said. I stuck out my hand to shake on it.

Justin beamed. "Really?"

"Whatever," I said. We shook.

I picked up my lunch tray and followed my friends to our table, trying to look like I didn't care. I took a big bite of the pizza and said, "Mmm," but the truth was I couldn't even taste it. My insides felt heavy, like they were already stuffed with cheese. Cold, lumpy cheese and regret.

I should never have gotten pulled into that big-mouth bet. This loose tooth was causing nothing but trouble.

Chapter Ten
Wiggle Away

On the way home from school I charged down
the sidewalk ahead of Chuck, wiggling my tooth
as hard as I could while I walked. I'd had more
than enough of this day already. I wanted to get
home to Banana.

"Yo, Anna, what's the rush?" my slowpoke
brother called from several feet behind me. "And
what are you doing in there, digging for gold?"

I whirled around. "I need to get this tooth
out," I said, walking backwards to keep moving.

Chuck sped up. "I bet I could knock it out
with my fist," he offered, grinning like he does

when he thinks he's being clever.

I rolled my eyes. "No thanks," I said, turning so I could walk forward again.

Chuck shuffled to keep up. "Want me to pull it out? Dad must have some pliers we could use."

"No!" I tried to elbow him in the side, but he ducked out of the way.

"You sure? It'd be easy. One little tug and . . . pop!"

My hand flew back to my mouth. I cupped my fingers over my jaw to protect it. "Keep your grubby paws away from me," I said into my hand. Chuck wouldn't really go after my tooth with pliers, but I squirmed a little even just thinking about it.

Chuck shrugged. "Suit yourself. You can keep it in forever, then."

I shook my head firmly. That was most definitely *not* an option. Especially now that Justin and the Funky Chicken were involved.

The faster I could get this tooth out, the sooner Justin would be forced to leave Isabel and Sadie and me alone. But I was sure that my tooth was already way looser than his. I wouldn't need Chuck's pliers to win.

Unless . . . what if Justin used pliers on *his*

tooth? I couldn't imagine anyone actually doing that, but with our bet on the line, it seemed almost possible.

I sped up and went back to the wiggling. Chuck groaned but sped up too.

I couldn't stop thinking about what Isabel had said about how the Tooth Fairy stops coming once you stop believing. Part of me was embarrassed for her that she thought that was true, but another big part of me wished I could snap my fingers and start believing again. I didn't want to be missing out on the magic. And even though it made sense that there might be no Tooth Fairy at all, I thought Isabel's theory made a lot of sense too.

But you can't just *decide* you believe in something. That's not how believing works. And if

I didn't fully, completely believe, the magic wouldn't work anyway, so I might as well not believe at all. Right?

I needed to discuss it with Banana. I kind of wanted to talk it over with Chuck, too, but I didn't want him to start joking about the Abominable Snowman and my imaginary friends, and talk me out of it. Chuck can be very persuasive. At least I knew Banana wouldn't laugh at me.

Maybe I could feel it out, though, without telling him the whole story. I looked at Chuck out of the corner of my eye. "Isabel still believes in the Tooth Fairy, even though I told her there's no such thing," I said.

Chuck shrugged. "So what?" he said.

That wasn't the response I'd been expecting. "So . . . don't you think that's embarrassing?"

"Is she embarrassed about it?" he asked.

I thought about that. No, I decided. She really wasn't. Isabel was hardly ever embarrassed about anything. I shook my head.

"Then why should you be embarrassed for her?" Chuck said.

"Because . . ." I started to say, but I didn't have a good answer. When he put it that way, I realized maybe I shouldn't.

Chapter Eleven

Loosen Up

What *would* be embarrassing, though, and surely get me in deep trouble, would be having to dance the Funky Chicken in the middle of class. I couldn't let that happen. I had to make sure my tooth fell out first. So I wiggled and wiggled and wiggled it.

I wiggled it with my left hand while doing homework with my right. I wiggled it with my

spoon while eating chocolate ice cream for dessert. I wiggled it with my tongue while Chuck and I cleared and washed the dishes. I wiggled it with my fingers while tossing Banana's favorite bunny toy, and patting her ears, and telling her about the bet, and explaining Isabel's ideas about the Tooth Fairy.

Banana wasn't sure about the Tooth Fairy stuff, but she was certain I'd be a superhero just like Sadie if I could win the bet and stop Justin from bothering us. She wiggled her entire backside to encourage my tooth along.

I wiggled the tooth until my fingers and wrists and elbows got tired, and my arms got sore, and the tooth got much looser. But even with all that wiggling it still wasn't quite loose enough.

"Maybe it will fall out while I'm sleeping," I whispered to Banana, in her basket, after Mom had tucked us in. Banana curled up into an even tighter ball and heaved a doggy sigh. We both would be relieved when this toothy trouble was over.

"Don't worry," I told her. "There's no way Justin's has fallen out yet either."

As I turned over to sleep on my other side, I gave the tooth one last, big good-night wiggle and hoped that was true.

Chapter Twelve
The Better Bettor

When I opened my eyes the next morning, Banana was already awake in her basket beside the bed, looking up at me with her ears perked in a question.

I touched my tongue to the tooth spot and shook my head. "Nope," I answered. "Still there."

Banana flattened her ears against her head and pushed her nose under her blanket with a sigh. That was how I felt about it too.

When Chuck and I got to school, Isabel and Sadie were waiting for me at the edge of the playground. Sadie ran over. "Justin's tooth is still in," she reported. "But he told some kid on the bus that he's certain it will come out today. How's yours?"

I showed them. Sadie grimaced. "We'll think of something," she promised. "But keep wiggling it."

All through school Justin was unusually quiet. He didn't tug my hair to get my attention during social studies, or try to tell any jokes before recess, or call out to tease Isabel or me or anyone else during silent reading time. He didn't even tap his pencil on his desk or ask to borrow my eraser during math. He kept his big mouth shut for once, which made me feel extra nervous because it probably meant he was too busy wiggling his tooth out to talk.

I couldn't know for sure what he was doing or not, though, because I refused to turn around and look. I kept my head facing forward and my eyes glued to the whiteboard, where Ms. Burland had written the word of the day, "foreboding." *Foreboding: a sense that something bad will happen.*

Yes. I was filled with exactly that.

When the final bell rang to release us from school, I popped out of my seat, turned toward

the coat hooks, and slammed straight into Justin. We both froze.

He looked at me with startled eyes for what felt like the longest second in the world. For a moment I wondered if Justin was filled with foreboding too. Maybe he was just as worried about the bet as I was.

Then he spoke. "Better rush home and practice your dance moves," he said, "since tomorrow you'll be performing in the middle of class. Bawk, bawk!"

I glared. "Better practice keeping your mouth shut," I said, "since soon you won't be allowed to open it at all."

I stormed off without waiting for his comeback. This tooth had to come out *now*.

Chapter Thirteen

Reality Bites

When Isabel and Sadie and I got to Sadie's house after school, my friends were ready with a plan.

"Chew this," Sadie said, handing me a pack of strawberry bubble gum. "It will pull the tooth right out."

I unwrapped three pieces of bubble gum and chewed them as best I could, while Sadie and Isabel took turns wearing the sparkly purple helmet and riding Sadie's new bike up and down her long driveway. I chewed while Isabel showed Sadie how to pop a wheelie in the grass. I chewed while Sadie tried it herself and Isabel cheered. I chewed until my jaw was sore and the big wad of gum had lost all its flavor. But the tooth stayed put.

Sadie put the bike away and led us into the kitchen, where she got me an apple. "Bite this," she said.

I took the apple and nodded, but I was a little bit scared. Biting into it with my loose tooth seemed like it might hurt. But I had to do it. I couldn't let Justin win the bet. I reminded myself that it wasn't just for my sake. I was doing this for my friends, too. I lifted the apple to my mouth.

"Wait," Sadie said. She got two more apples,

one for her and one for Isabel. "We'll do it together. On the count of three. One . . . two . . . three!"

With my friends beside me, I could be extra brave. I chomped into the apple and felt my tooth move, but it didn't come out. I took another bite and felt it again. But still the tooth stayed in.

Sadie's plan wasn't working.

Sadie frowned. Isabel looked worried. They glanced at each other, then back at me, and Isabel swallowed hard.

"There's one more thing we haven't tried," Sadie said. "But it's pretty drastic. I don't think you should do it."

"What is it?" I asked.

Sadie turned to Isabel. "Tell her," she said.

Isabel shifted from one foot to the other and back again. I'd never seen her so nervous. "Well," she said. "I don't know if this is true, but my sister Emma knows a girl who says her brother once pulled his tooth out by tying it to a doorknob."

"You mean, like, with a piece of string?" I said, trying to picture it.

Isabel nodded gravely. "And then slamming the door shut," she said.

I blinked. "Oh," I said, feeling the breath whoosh out of me.

Nobody moved.

Part of me wanted to run home and bury my face in Banana's soft fur and forget about the tooth and the bet and especially about Justin. But another part of me, the same part that had gotten me into this dumb bet in the first place, wanted something different. That part of me wanted to be the kind of person who would do something huge to protect my friends. Something drastic. Something brave.

I stood taller. I wanted to be a superhero. "I'll do it," I said.

Chapter Fourteen
All Tied Up

Isabel's eyebrows shot up. "Are you sure?" she said.

"You don't have to," Sadie told me. Now she looked worried too—as worried as Banana gets when Dad turns on the vacuum.

I shook my head to clear away their questions. "I'm sure," I said. "Let's try it."

I wanted to do it quickly, before I could change my mind.

My stomach flipped and spun in a crazy dance while Sadie ran to get a spool of dental floss. She pulled off a long string of it and handed the string to Isabel. I opened my mouth wide. Isabel carefully tied one end of the floss to my tooth, and the other end to the pantry door.

I reminded myself that this would all be over in a few seconds, and tried to picture how excited Banana would get when she heard my tooth was out before Justin's. I imagined how grateful my friends would be to go the whole rest of the year without him annoying any of us. I did *not* think about what it would feel like when the door slammed shut and the string yanked my tooth and the blood gushed out. But even without letting myself think about that, my heart was pounding fast.

"Okay, on the count of three I'm going to slam the door. Are you ready?" Sadie said.

I nodded as well as I could with my jaw hanging open and my tooth tied to a doorknob. A doorknob that was about to rip the tooth right out.

"One . . . " Sadie said.

I took a deep breath. Isabel grabbed my hand.

"Two . . . " Sadie said.

I squeezed Isabel's hand and shut my eyes tight. I didn't want to look, and I didn't want to cry. I hoped I wouldn't pass out.

I wondered how we'd stop the bleeding.

"Th—"

"Wait!" I cried, lunging to grab the door before Sadie could push it. "I can't do it."

I watched through a blur of tears and relief as Isabel quickly untied the doorknob. I slipped the other end of the floss off my tooth and sank to the floor in defeat.

"I'm sorry," I said. "I'm so, so sorry."

My friends dropped to the floor beside me and wrapped me in a double hug.

"Don't be sorry," Sadie said. "You were so brave to even think about doing that. I wouldn't have."

"Yeah," Isabel said. "Why are you apologizing?"

"Because I might lose the bet," I said, wiping my drippy eyes. "And this is our chance to make Justin leave us alone. I don't want to let you guys down."

Isabel looked surprised. "You're not letting us down," she said. "We're just trying to help save you from having to do the Funky Chicken. It's okay with us if you don't win. We can still handle Justin. I don't care what he thinks."

Sadie was nodding. "Besides, sometimes Justin's funny," she said. "And kind of cute," she added.

I wrinkled my nose. That was grosser than a dog fart.

"Anyway, you don't have to do this for *us*," Sadie said. "We love you no matter what."

That was nice to hear, and it did make me feel better, but it didn't solve all my worries. Losing wouldn't only mean blowing my chance to make Justin leave us alone. It would also mean having to act out in class, like some kind of troublemaker. Ms. Burland would be so disappointed in me. And when she called my parents to tell them what I'd done, my parents would be disappointed too. I'd probably get detention *and* be grounded for life.

Isabel brushed some dirt off her sneaker. "You know, if you lose, you don't have to go through with that chicken dance," she said. "We can tell Justin you're not doing it."

Sadie and I stared at her like she was crazy, because apparently, she was. "Of course I do," I said. "Everyone heard us make the bet. And we shook on it. I can't back out now."

Isabel shrugged. "It just doesn't seem very smart," she said.

I nodded sadly. "It's definitely not smart."

Sadie crossed her arms. "Well, you haven't lost yet. And maybe you won't. But if you do, we'll just have to outsmart him."

"Okay," I said, feeling a little more hopeful. "How?"

Sadie looked at Isabel, then back at me. "I have no idea," she admitted. "But we'll think of something. We always do."

Chapter Fifteen
The Biggest Loser

The next morning I woke up certain: Today was the day my tooth would come out. It was super loose and twisty, and barely holding on at all. I was going to beat Justin and win the bet. I just knew it.

I threw on my favorite polka-dot dress and a pair of stripey leggings, and ran down the stairs with Banana right behind me.

"Still got that tooth in, kiddo?" Dad asked as we came into the kitchen.

"Yup, but not for long," I said.

I scooped some kibble into

Banana's food dish and served her a kiss on the snout. "Did you ever figure out your book's big plot twist?" I asked him.

Dad smiled over the top of his TOP DOG coffee mug. "Yes, actually."

"What is it?" I said, reaching for the box of Gorilla Grams.

"Everything will turn out the way the heroine wanted. But when it does, she'll realize that maybe that wasn't what she truly wanted after all," Dad said, sounding pleased with himself.

I glanced at Banana. She didn't think that was a very good plot twist either.

"Oh," I said. When my tooth fell out first and I won the bet like I wanted, I was *not* going to realize I'd really wanted it to go another way. But I didn't tell Dad that his plot twist sounded dumb.

That wouldn't be polite, and I'm not old enough for his books yet anyway.

When I got to school, Sadie and Isabel were waiting, ready to give me the Tooth Report. "Justin's is still in," Sadie said. "He wiggled it the entire bus ride, but it hasn't come out yet."

I showed them how loose mine was. Isabel let out a squeal. "You're way far ahead of him! You'll win today for sure."

"Thanks to the gum and the apple," I said.

Sadie grinned. "What are friends for?"

But when we walked into the classroom, our smiles disappeared fast. A whole bunch of kids were crowded around Justin's desk. Justin stood next to it, holding a bloody tissue to his mouth. When he saw me, he said, "There she is!" He held out his hand to show me the tooth that was lying in his palm.

I couldn't believe it. I'd lost the bet.

"Bawk, bawk!" Justin said. "Time to dance!"

I gulped and turned away. My stomach felt sick. What had I gotten myself into?

"She's not really going to do it," I heard Amanda say. "She'll wimp out for sure."

"She can't," Timothy said. "They shook on it."

Sadie gripped my arm. "We'll dance it with you," she said. "You don't have to do this alone."

Isabel was nodding, but I shook my head. There was no reason for all three of us to get in big trouble. I was the one who'd made the stupid bet and gotten myself into this mess in the first place. Now I'd have to dance my way out of it.

But as my Nana would say, I might have bitten off more than I could chew.

Chapter Sixteen
Chickening Out

The bell rang and everyone scrambled into their seats as Ms. Burland clapped twice to start the day. I was so nervous, I could hardly see straight.

Ms. Burland was the very best teacher I'd ever had, but she was pretty strict. If I stood up in class and started flapping and bawking, there was no way she wouldn't be furious. Even though I'd heard her say, "Learning should be fun," I didn't think she'd find my dance very funny. The only learning involved would be me learning how it feels to be in deep, deep trouble.

My stomach hurt. I needed a distraction. I focused on the whiteboard, where Ms. Burland had written the word of the day. Today's word was "zany": *silly in an unexpected, out-of-the-ordinary way.*

There was nothing zany about the way I felt. "Pukey" would be a better word for that.

I wished I could whistle for Banana to come save me.

I stared down at the floor as Ms. Burland handed back our spelling quizzes from earlier in the week. She was wearing her bright-green shoes with neon-pink laces that I love. Last time she wore those, Sadie had called them the Watermelon Shoes. Banana had thought that sounded delicious.

The shoes went well with today's word of the day. Ms. Burland had zany watermelon feet.

Wait. That's it! I thought. Suddenly I knew exactly how to outsmart Justin, and maybe get in slightly less trouble.

I shot my hand up into the air. "Ms. Burland," I said. "Ms. Burland!" I had to do this quickly, while she was still passing back the quizzes. And before I lost my nerve.

"Yes, Anna?" she said.

I stood up. This was it.

In as calm and loud a voice as I could manage while my stomach was turning in circles like Banana chasing her tail, I announced, "I'd like to demonstrate the word of the day. Here's my *zany* dance, the Funky Chicken!"

I tucked my hands under my armpits and flapped my elbows, lifting my knees one at a time and squawking, "Bawk, bawk, bawk!" as I danced down the aisle and back. "Bawk, bawk!"

When I reached my desk again, I stopped and stood still. The classroom was completely silent. I could feel my cheeks burning and everyone staring at me in total surprise, but I couldn't look at any of my classmates. I had to look at Ms. Burland, to see how much trouble I was in.

Ms. Burland's face was frozen in shock. She lifted her hand to her forehead, and then . . . she laughed!

I couldn't believe it. I broke into a huge smile as everyone around me laughed too.

Ms. Burland shook her head. "That was silly and unexpected indeed, Anna. Very zany. I'm glad you're so excited about the word of the day. But next time you'd like to act one out, please talk to me first, so we can schedule it not to disrupt, okay?"

"Okay," I said.

"Now, if everyone's done dancing and could take a seat, let's talk about next week's spelling words." She turned toward the board to write.

I couldn't believe my luck. I'd done it! I'd out-smarted Justin and gotten away with the dance. I couldn't wait to tell Banana the whole tale.

I peeked over at Isabel and Sadie. Their faces glowed with triumph. Sadie flashed me a big thumbs-up.

Before I slid into my seat, I looked straight at Justin. I expected him to be mad or maybe even try to say that it somehow didn't count. But to my surprise, Justin was smiling too. "That was awesome!" he whispered. He held out his hand for a high five. "I can't believe you did it!"

As my palm hit his, I smiled back.

Maybe Justin wasn't always so bad after all.

Chapter Seventeen
Nothing Left to Lose

When I got home from school, Banana was waiting by the door. She was eager to hear the State of the Teeth and ready for our walk. "I lost the bet," I told her, and she stared up at me with big, worried eyes. "But I also won," I said. She blinked in surprise and lifted her ears.

I shrugged off my backpack and clipped on her leash. "Come on," I said. "I'll tell you all about it." We bounded out the door.

I told her the whole story as we started down the sidewalk, stopping a few times so I could act out the good parts. Banana jumped and danced at my feet while I showed her how I'd flapped and squawked through the Funky Chicken. When I got to the part about Justin's high five, she barked and held up her paw. I was laughing and high-pawing her back when I suddenly felt something there on my tongue.

I'd finally lost the tooth!

I stuck my tongue out so Banana could see. Her tail shot straight up.

I inspected the tooth and closed my fingers around it, remembering everything that Isabel had said. *Tooth Fairy, Tooth Fairy,* I thought, letting the hope bubble up inside me. I couldn't help it—I wanted to believe.

"Let's go tell Dad," I said. But when I tugged Banana's leash, she didn't budge.

"What?" I asked. She looked at me. "Ohhh," I said, slowly catching on. "Good point."

Banana was right. If I showed Dad the tooth, then he and Mom would step in for the Tooth Fairy tonight. But if I didn't tell them—if I kept it quiet and put the tooth under my pillow and hoped and wished and believed—then maybe, just maybe, the Tooth Fairy would come herself. I had to try it.

Banana wagged her tail as I dropped the tooth into my polka-dot pocket. "Okay," I said. "It's our secret."

Chapter Eighteen
These Lips Are Sealed

Keeping the tooth a secret sounded easy at first, but Banana and I soon realized it was going to be tricky. It wasn't just a matter of not showing anyone the tooth. I also had to make sure they didn't see the gap in my mouth where the tooth was missing. That meant I'd need to be pretty sneaky.

All through dinner I kept my lips sealed as much as I could. I answered "mm-hmm" for yes or "mm-mmm" for no, and made extra sure to chew with my mouth closed. The one time I really *had* to speak, when Mom asked about my day, I thought fast and held my napkin up to my face, pretending to wipe my mouth while I talked. I kept the answer as short as possible, and no one seemed to notice.

Banana stayed by my chair, standing guard just in case, but I didn't even need her for backup. We were getting away with it! I snuck her a small piece of tofu from my stir-fry, and she looked up at me happily.

After dinner Chuck and I cleared the table, and I hummed the tune of one of Isabel's silly songs so no one would think I was being too quiet. Chuck started humming too, a different tune on top of mine, trying to mess me up. I hummed a little louder, so he hummed louder too, and soon we were both buzzing at top volume in a Great Hum-Off. The giggles were building and building in my throat, but I kept up the humming and Chuck broke first. We both burst out laughing, and I covered my mouth with my hand. He didn't suspect a thing.

When the dishes were done, we all went into the living room to watch a funny show. I curled up on the couch next to Dad, and Banana jumped up too. She put her head on my lap so I could tug her silky ears. It was easier to keep my tooth secret then, since the lights were off. You're not supposed to talk during a show anyway, though of course Chuck still did.

Dad clicked off the television at the end of the night. "All right, kiddos, time for bed. Go brush those teeth and get in your pajamas, and Mom will be up to tuck you in soon."

"One more show," Chuck begged. "Pleeeeeeease?"

But Banana and I jumped off the couch and ran upstairs.

"We did it!" I said, squeezing her in a hug. There was only one challenge left.

When we heard Mom's footsteps in the hallway a few minutes later, we were ready. Banana was in her basket and I was already in bed with the lights off. I rolled over onto my side, facing the wall, so the part of my mouth with the gap in it was buried in the pillow. I'd taken the secret tooth out of my polka-dot pocket and was holding it in my right hand, hidden safely under the covers, along with a note that I'd written. The note said, *Dear Tooth Fairy: I believe.*

As Mom came in, I crossed the fingers on my left hand for luck.

Mom sat on the bed and put her hand on my back, rubbing it gently like she does during tuck-ins. "You were pretty quiet at dinner tonight, Annabear. Everything okay?"

I nodded into the pillow. "Yup," I said. "Just tired."

"Are you nervous about your loose tooth?" she asked.

"No," I said honestly. Well, sort of honestly. I was nervous about the tooth—about hiding it, and about whether the Tooth Fairy would come. But I wasn't nervous about a *loose* tooth. I was worried about a tooth that had already fallen out. But I couldn't tell Mom any of that until tomorrow.

"Good. I'm sure it will come out soon," she said.

"And then I'll be more like Banana," I said.

"You will?" Mom asked.

"Yup," I said. "Dad said that kind of tooth is called a canine tooth, and 'canine' means 'dog.' So when the little canine tooth falls out, and an even bigger one grows in, that means I'll be that much more doggy, like Banana."

Mom laughed. "I hadn't thought of it that way, but it's a good theory," she said. "Sleep tight, my little doggies."

She kissed me first and then Banana, and shut the door firmly behind her.

I pulled my hand out from under the blanket and gave the tooth one last squeeze for luck. Then I slipped it and the note under my pillow so the Tooth Fairy could find it.

"Good night," I whispered to Banana.

I heard her tail go *thump, thump, thump*.

Chapter Nineteen

Fairy Certain

I thought I'd be too excited to sleep, wondering if the Tooth Fairy would come. But the next thing I knew, the morning sunlight was sneaking in through the window blinds and making stripes across my bed. I blinked a few times, still slowly waking up. Until suddenly I remembered, and my heart raced in double time.

I held my breath and slid a hand under the pillow, almost afraid of what I'd find. My finger hit something hard. Something hard that was *not my tooth*.

"It worked!" I cried, startling Banana awake. "The magic worked!"

Banana wriggled out of her basket, fast. She put her front paws up on the mattress so she could see too.

I lifted up my pillow. There, underneath it, were two silver dollars, a unicorn-shaped eraser, and a dog treat for Banana.

Sadie wouldn't believe it. But Isabel definitely would. I couldn't wait to tell them both.

I kissed Banana's snout and whispered, "Do you think it's really real?"

Banana licked the tip of my nose. I giggled and wiped it off with my arm. She jumped down off the bed and went to stand by the door.

I'd bet anything that what Banana really thought was, *I believe it's time for breakfast.*

Acknowledgments

A toothy grin of thanks to the whole team at S&S, especially editor Kristin Ostby, for her sharp eye, smart brain, and chicken dance know-how; and designer Laurent Linn, who, together with Meg Park, makes these books look adorable.

A tail wag and a grateful lick to my agent, Meredith Kaffel Simonoff, who works more magic than the Tooth Fairy.

Thank you Robin Wasserman, chief strategist, who helped give this plot bite, and Terra Elan McVoy, who kept me from pulling out my teeth through the process.

I wrote this book while in a lot of pretty places: Brooklyn, Princeton, Nassau, Greenstone, Miami, Delray Beach, Waterford, and Deer Isle. Thanks to the friends and family who were in those places with me.

Hey, Jeff: wiggle wiggle.

Arugula Badidea, you are the funkiest chicken of all.

Here's a sneak peek at

ANNA, BANANA, AND THE PUPPY PARADE

Anna, Banana, and the Puppy Parade

Anica Mrose Rissi   ILLUSTRATED BY Meg Park

Would You Rather

"Okay, I've got one," my best friend Sadie said. "Would you rather have your own magic unicorn, but you have to keep it a secret, or have a regular horse that isn't magic but everyone can know about it?"

"The unicorn," my other best friend, Isabel, said immediately. "Who wouldn't choose the unicorn?"

Sadie swallowed a mouthful of her peanut-butter banana sandwich. "I wouldn't. I'd choose the horse so I could ride him to school and show him off to people and stuff. Horses aren't magic but they're still beautiful." She looked at me. "What about you, Anna?"

I chewed a slice of apple while I thought. This

was a hard one. Sadie was really good at this game. "I'm not sure," I said. "I'd love to have a unicorn, but I can't keep secrets from Banana." Banana always seems to know what I'm thinking. That's part of what makes her the best dog ever.

Sadie grinned. "Telling Banana wouldn't count."

"Okay, but I'd also want to tell you guys," I said. "So I choose the horse." I pictured the three of us riding through a field on a chestnut mare. We'd braid her mane and brush her coat until it shone, and I'd always keep sugar cubes in my pockets for her. The best part of having a horse would be sharing her with my friends.

"My turn," Isabel said. "Would you rather be a famous actress or a famous singer?"

"Actress!" Sadie said.

"Singer," I said.

"Me too. We can sing duets," Isabel said to me.

"Hey, then I want to be a singer too!" Sadie said. "No, wait. I'll still be a famous actress and you guys can sing the soundtracks for all my movies."

"Deal," Isabel said.

It was my turn to ask a question next. I looked around the lunchroom for inspiration. "Hmm. Would you rather look like a troll but smell like roses, or be super pretty but always smell like the school cafeteria on hot dog day?"

"Ew!" Sadie said. We all burst into giggles.

Banana loves hot dogs, which is funny because she's also shaped like one, all long and skinny in the middle. The hot dogs we eat at home are tasty, but today's hot lunch smelled like ketchup and skunk stew.

At least the ketchup came in packets instead of squeeze bottles, so we didn't have to listen to ketchup farts while we ate. My brother gets those bottles to make the grossest sounds possible. He's disgustingly good at it.

"I'd be a nice-smelling troll, definitely," Isabel said when she'd caught her breath.

Sadie scrunched up her nose and shook her head. Her curls bounced. "I can't answer this one," she said.

"We'd still love you if you smelled like school lunch," I promised her.

"We'd just love you from a little farther away," Isabel teased.

Sadie stuck out her tongue. She folded up

her sandwich wrapper and wiped her lips with a paper napkin. As usual, Sadie's side of the table was much neater than Isabel's and mine. Though most of the mess on our side was Isabel's.

Isabel stuffed her own trash into her lunchbox. "Oh! I almost forgot," she said, pulling out a piece of paper. "I brought you a surprise." She smoothed out the wrinkles and thrust the paper at me. "Ta-da!"

Paws on Parade

I took the light-blue paper from Isabel's hand and saw the word PUPPY on it, upside-down, in all capital letters. Before I could even turn the page right-side up, Sadie was leaning across the table to look. "What is it?" she asked.

I read it out loud. "'Calling all pups for the Puppy Parade! Paws, prizes, treats, tail-wagging, music, and more.'"

Isabel shimmied in her seat. "It's perfect, right? They were handing them out at the grocery store," she said.

"Let me see," Sadie said. She pulled the paper out of my hands.

"Hey! I wasn't finished," I told her.

"Sorry." She handed it back. Sadie can be

pretty bossy sometimes, even with her friends, but I'm learning to stand up for myself when I need to.

I kept reading. "'Bring your family and your fabulous furry friend for a day of fun at the Happy Homes Animal Shelter's first annual dog show. Parade starts at the east entrance of Piddleton Park at 10 am sharp. Refreshments provided by Rosie's Bakery and Yip Yap Yums.'" I looked up at my friends. "That's the shelter where we got Banana. This sounds like so much fun!"

Sadie reached for the flier again and this time I let her take it.

"You have to enter Banana," Isabel said. "She'll win for sure."

Sadie was nodding. "Banana is definitely Best in Show," she said. Best in Show was the top prize in the dog show Sadie and I watched on TV last year, back before we met Isabel. We'd seen so many cute dogs, all fancily groomed and well behaved—but no dog was as special as Banana, I thought. I was glad to hear my friends agreed.

I imagined Banana in a sparkly gold collar, marching past the judges with her ears perked and her tail in the air. I pictured myself in a matching gold headband, holding Banana's leash and smiling proudly as the crowd gasped at her cuteness. Banana would be a star. And that would make me a star too.

"'Saturday the twelfth,'" Sadie read. "That's this weekend. We only have two days to get ready!"

We? I hadn't pictured Sadie and Isabel being in the parade too—I'd assumed it would just be Banana and me. But of course Sadie and Isabel would walk with us. It would be even more fun with my best friends by my side. I'd still be the one holding the leash though, so everyone would know that Banana is my dog.

"Good thing we're having a sleepover at your house tomorrow," Sadie said, pushing the flier back across the table. "There's so much to do. We need to start planning right away."

"We do?" I said. I was excited about the parade and the sleepover too, but I wasn't sure what kind of planning Sadie had in mind.

"Yes!" Sadie jumped up as the bell rang. The cafeteria filled with the clanging and banging of kids all around us rushing to bus their trays. "I'll make a to-do list and write down ideas."

"And I'll help!" Isabel said. as she and Sadie started for the door.

I grabbed my lunch bag and hurried after them, feeling weirdly left out. Banana was *my* dog. Why was Sadie in charge of the parade plans? "Then what am I supposed to do?" I asked when I'd caught up.

"You'll add ideas too," Sadie said. "We're all in this together, right?"

"Right!" Isabel cheered, and I realized I was being silly. They weren't trying to take over. They just wanted to be part of the fun.

"Right," I echoed. Sadie hooked her arms through Isabel's and mine, and we skipped down the hall back to class.